From Heathers Acre Farm

Ave Rosche 11/21/04

# The
# BLUE RIBBON
# ALPACA

by
Susan
Rosche

Illustrations
by
Tamra Davis

# Dedication

To Don, Katy and Ben,
with love

In loving memory of my Dad
"Pop Pop Heyman"

Design and production by Bruce Taylor Hamilton

ISBN 0-9752566-0-2

Copyright © 2004

## PAX RIVER ALPACAS PUBLISHING

Upper Marlboro, Maryland

*Publishing*

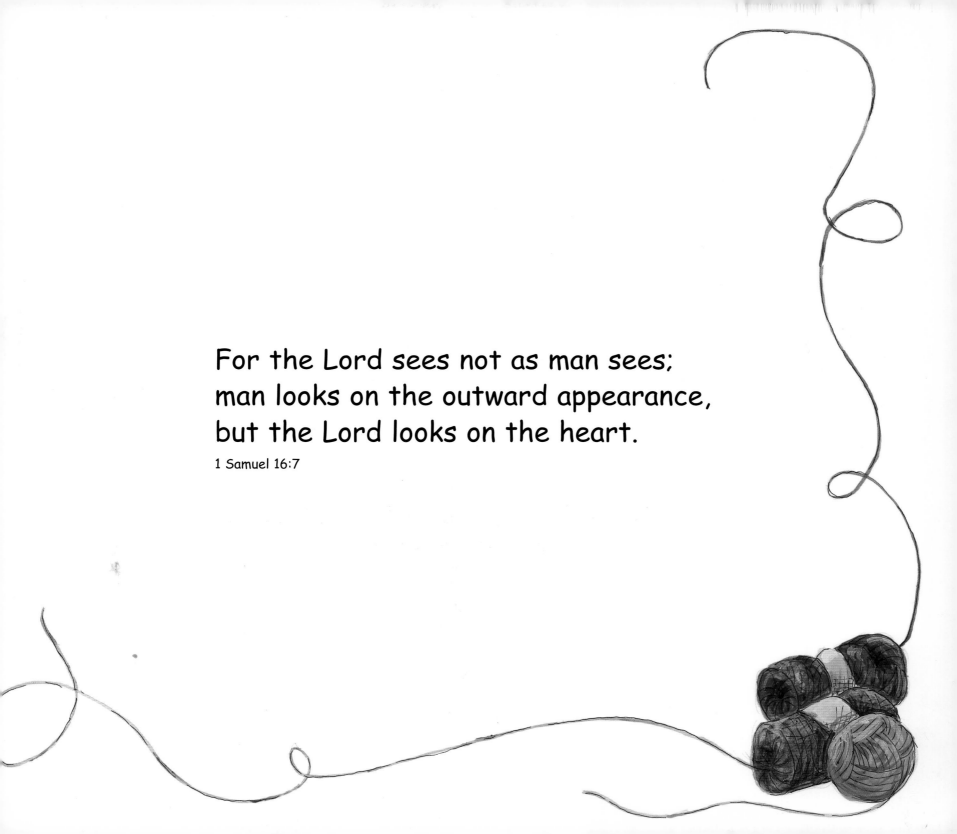

For the Lord sees not as man sees;
man looks on the outward appearance,
but the Lord looks on the heart.

1 Samuel 16:7

Josephine was born one frosty November morning. She lay on the ground for a long time, wet and shivering. "Get up Josephine, please get up," her mother pleaded. Josephine tried her best, making it halfway up, but fell back down. She was so weak she could barely move. She felt helpless and scared. "Josephine, you must keep trying." Her mother was frantic. Josephine could no longer move. She could barely hear her mother crying, "Please don't die!"

Suddenly Josephine felt herself lifted up into strong arms. "She's still alive," cried a voice as a towel was wrapped around her. She was rushed into the warm barn with her mother running alongside.

"She's adorable," cried the three children who waited for her inside. They dried her, warmed her, and gave her a bottle, sin her mother didn't have any milk. Soon Josephine started to fe much better. She gently hummed as the children rubbed her long neck. "You're going to make it Josephine, you'll be all right her mother whispered softly as she gently nuzzled her face.

By afternoon Josephine was able to stand. "Yippee," she yelled as she took off running across the pasture, kicking her rear legs high into the air. The children squealed with delight. That night she snuggled close to her mother. It had been a long day.

very day, Don, the oldest, came to the barn to give Josephine her bottle. Katy
nd Ben always followed close behind. Sometimes they carried her into the
arm house where she was the center
f attention. While inside, Josephine
stened as the family talked about how
uch they loved their prize-winning
lpacas. She decided she too must become
champion in order to earn their love.

Before long, Josephine was no longer brought into the house. She munched grass in the pasture and listened as the other alpacas talked about all the ribbons they had won. They were very proud of themselves. "I can't wait until I'm old enough to win a ribbon," thought Josephine. "Then the kids will love me forever."

The children came to the pasture every day to care for the alpacas. Josephine followed them everywhere and helped as they herded the alpacas into the barn. "Josephine, you are the world's sweetest alpaca," they said as they hugged her and rubbed her neck. She was proud to be so helpful. But not everyone appreciated her help. "Who does she think she is, herding us into the barn," complained Morning Glory.

the years passed, Josephine
...ited for her chance to
...mpete in a show. Finally,
...th a heavy heart, she
...mitted what she
...ared to be true.
...'m not good enough
... win a ribbon. I'm
...thing but a failure."
...sephine looked at
...er reflection in the
...ter bucket. A long,
...k face stared back
...her. A face with eyes
...at always looked like
...ey had been crying.
...e shook her head to
...ff up the scraggly
...pknot that covered it,
...t it was no use. Soon
...e children would see
...e truth and stop loving
...r. Josephine plopped down
... a heap and sobbed.

Every spring the alpacas left the farm to compete in the big show. Josephine watched longingly as they got ready. They were so straight and proud. Their enormous eyes and dazzling colors gleamed in the sunlight. "Look how plain you are Josephine", said Silver Bell as she pranced around the barn. Josephine was surprised at Silver Bell's behavior.

While the other alpacas were at the big show, a man came to the farm to shear Josephine. When he finished, he put her fleece in a special box. Josephine itched like crazy. She felt skinny and ugly. Her curved back looked even rounder. "Why does that man cut my fleece so short?" she complained.

Josephine

When the alpacas returned with their many ribbons, they too had been shorn. Josephine inspected each one of them, but no one had their fleece cut as short as hers.

One warm, sunny day while Josephine was sitting, cushed in the pasture, her owners brought home one of the most beautiful alpacas she had ever seen. "That's Celosa," said Nestle. "She is undefeated." Celosa's thick fleece was such a soft, lovely shade of gray that it blended in with the tiny lavender flowers growing in the pasture. All the alpacas admired Celosa and she quickly became the most popular alpaca on the farm.

But, it wasn't long until Celosa became quite rude to Josephine. Josephine tried to be extra nice to her, but things only got worse. One day while they were eating, Celosa shoved Josephine out of the way and spit in her face. "The kids don't like you anymore. They only like the finest alpacas." Josephine tried to ignore her, but it really hurt her feelings.

Josephine tried to avoid Celosa,
but Celosa would not leave her alone.
"Your fleece was cut so short because it is ugly,"
Celosa told her. Soon
the other alpacas joined
in and began to tease
Josephine too. But
even worse, the chil–
dren had not been to
the barn for days.

The days slowly turned into weeks and the teasing didn't stop, nor did the children come. Josephine decided Celosa was right. Her worst fear was coming true; the children could see she was worthless and no longer loved her.

That night Josephine could
not sleep. "I must win back
the children's love." After
several long hours, she
noticed the barn office
door was open. A shiny,
blue ribbon inside caught
her eye. It was hanging
over the back of a chair.
This gave her an idea.

She got up carefully and tiptoed into the office. When she nudged the ribbon, it slid easily over her neck.

Josephine admired herself in the mirror, pretending the ribbon was hers. Suddenly there in the doorway stood Prudence - the oldest and wisest alpaca on the farm. Josephine gasped. "Josephine, what on earth are you doing?" Josephine started shaking. Prudence was the leader of the herd. All the alpacas respected her.

Prudence started to scold Josephine until she noticed tears streaming down her face. "The children don't love me anymore, "Josephine sobbed. "How do you know this?" asked Prudence. Josephine repeated what Celosa had said. "Do you know why she is being unkind?" asked Prudence. "Because I am worthless. I can't even win a ribbon," Josephine cried. "Josephine, love is not something that is earned!"

Prudence motioned for Josephine to follow her. "Come, I want to show you something."

rudence led Josephine
to a room she had never
en before. When Jose-
hine peered inside she
uld hardly believe her
es. Dozens of beautiful
weaters hung all over
e wall. "Touch them." Jose-
hine rubbed her cheek against
sweater. It was the softest
ing she ever felt,
en softer than her Mommy
en she was a cria. "They're
autiful," she sighed.

"Josephine!" Prudence said, "These sweaters were all made from your fleece. You have the most beautiful fleece in the world. Look at their labels." Josephine nudged a sweater. "Why it says Josephine!" She quickly nudged another. "This one says Josephine too." "Yes Josephine," said Prudence. "You are famous. People come from all over to buy "Josephine" sweaters. The alpacas are very, very jealous of you."

Then she noticed a wall covered with big, shiny blue ribbons. If only she could win such a ribbon. Prudence shook her head. "Silly girl, these are your ribbons. Your fleece won them all. You have won more ribbons than any other alpaca on the farm." Josephine looked puzzled. "Then why have the children stopped visiting me?" Prudence laughed. "They have been on vacation. They'll be back tomorrow."

The next day, Josephine's ears perked up when she heard her owner's car pull in the driveway. Ben jumped out and ran over to her, giving her hugs and kisses. Then he showed her the biggest, shiniest blue ribbon she had ever seen. "Guess what, Josephine? Your fleece won this ribbon at the great big show. Someone wanted to buy you, but Mommy told them that you are part of our family."

Ben hung the ribbon around Josephine's neck as he whispered in her ear. "Do you want to know a secret? You're my most favorite alpaca in the whole world. I wish you weren't a world champion, cause I don't want to have to share you with anyone!"

The other kids ran up to Josephine, grabbed her
around the neck and hugged her so tightly she
could hardly breathe. Then suddenly Katy stood
back and took a good look at Josephine. "Mommy,
look at Josephine! She looks different!"
Josephine stood straight and proud,
her big eyes shone brightly as she smiled.

# ABOUT ALPACAS

The alpaca, a member of the camelid family, is native to the Andes Mountains in South America, primarily Bolivia, Chile and Peru. Alpacas have flourished there for thousands of years. During the reign of the Incas, only high-ranking officials and nobility were privileged to wear the highly prized, exquisite alpaca fiber. Alpaca is a specialty fiber that is stronger, lighter, warmer and softer than sheep's wool and doesn't itch.

An alpaca is about half the size of a llama and can weigh between 100-225 lbs. There are two types of alpacas—the huacaya (wa-cai-ah) and the suri (sir-e). The huacaya has dense, yet soft and fluffy fleece with a thick puff of fleece on its head called the topknot. Their fiber has a crimp or wave, which enhances its weaving and spinning properties. The suri has long fleece that falls down at its sides in either curly, twisted or straight locks. The suri's topknot looks almost like a long toupee. Suri fiber is known for its wonderful luster, or shine. An alpaca's fleece keeps it warm in the cold, dry in the rain, and protects it from the sun.

Alpacas were first introduced to the U.S. in 1984. They have become increasingly popular ever since. Many alpaca owners enter their alpacas in shows where they are judged for various qualities such as: the softness, density and coverage of their fleece; their posture and the way they carry themselves; their agility and demeanor. They also enter their (shorn) fleeces in fiber shows where the best fibers are awarded ribbons. If an alpaca has a high quality fleece but lacks the physical qualities to be competitive in the show ring, it can still compete in the fiber show.

Alpacas are very friendly, gentle animals. They are easy to care for, disease resistant, odor free and do well in most climates. They are not aggressive and don't bite. Alpacas spit at each other as part of their communication, but don't often spit at humans. They are a herd animal and do not do well alone. Alpacas are very curious and intelligent. Most will let you get very close to them, but back away when you try to touch them, although some are very sociable and love for you to rub their necks. They generally don't like to have their heads petted. Alpacas that have to be bottle fed when they are crias usually become very friendly. It is not common to bottle feed an alpaca cria, but occasionally the mother may not produce enough milk or on rare occasions the mother may die at birth.

Raising alpacas is truly a rewarding experience that involves the entire family. It can also be a very profitable investment and an enjoyable and satisfying home business.

## ALPACA TERMS

| | |
|---|---|
| Cria (cree-ah): | a baby alpaca |
| Cush: | the way an alpaca sits on all fours similar to a camel |
| Fleece: | the "fur" on an alpaca |
| Herd: | a group of alpacas |
| Huacaya (wa-cai-ah): | a breed of alpaca with thick, fluffy fleece that puffs out like cotton candy and gives it a teddy bear/soft cuddly appearance. |
| Shear: | to cut the fleece off an alpaca |
| Shorn: | an alpaca after its fleece has been cut |
| Suri (sir-e): | a breed of alpaca with long fleece that falls down at its sides in either curly, twisted or straight locks. |
| Top Knot: | the fleece on top of an alpaca's head |

## ABOUT THE AUTHOR

*The Blue Ribbon Alpaca* evolved from one of the many bedtime alpaca stories Susan tells her children, Katy and Ben. Alpacas naturally lend themselves to an array of stories, given their teddy bear like appearance, gentle demeanor and distinct personalities. Alpaca stories have continued to be a favorite in the Rosche house ever since Susan and husband Don started Pax River Alpacas, an alpaca breeding business in southern Maryland. The Rosche's have found alpaca breeding to be a wonderfully enriching experience that involves the entire family and has helped teach the children responsibility and self-confidence.

The Rosches welcome visitors to their farm, located near the Patuxent River in Upper Marlboro, Maryland and to their website at www.paxriveralpacas.com

## ABOUT THE ILLUSTRATOR

Tamra (Wudtke) Davis specializes in commissioned art-work. Illustrating *The Blue Ribbon Alpaca* was Tamra's first experience with alpacas. She is fascinated with these lovely creatures and has enjoyed capturing their distinct behaviors, characteristics and individual personalities in her artwork Tamra lives near Sioux Falls, South Dakota with her husband Tim, a Lutheran Pastor, and their three sons, Issac, Isaiah and Gideon, to whom she credits her success.